THE LIFE AND OPINIONS OF TRISTRAM SHANDY, GENTLEMAN

The Life and Opinions of
TRISTRAM SHANDY,
GENTLEMAN

MARTIN ROWSON

THE OVERLOOK PRESS
WOODSTOCK · NEW YORK

First published in the United States in 1997 by
The Overlook Press, Peter Mayer Publishers, Inc.
Lewis Hollow Road
Woodstock, New York 12498

Library of Congress Cataloging-in-Publication Data

Rowson, Martin.
The life and opinions of Tristram Shandy, gentleman / Martin Rowson.
p.   cm.
I. Sterne, Laurence, 1713-1768.   Life and Opinions of
Tristram Shandy, gentleman. II. Title.
PN6727.R69L54   1997   741.5973--dc21   96-49506

Manufactured in United States of America

Originally published in Great Britain by Picador,
an imprint of Macmillan Publishers Ltd

ISBN 0-87951-768-9
FIRST AMERICAN EDITION
1 3 5 7 9 8 6 4 2

To the following good and great personages am I most humbly indebted, for their help, guidance and (if you please) forbearance, though never any poor jackass in the kingdom deserved it less—and I hope to the heavens (and back again) that, howsoever ill kempt it appear, its wig unpowdered, its coat damp and a nest of *cuckoos* in its cap and bells—they accept—I shall think myself the happiest man alive if they do—my poor thanks:

Dr Marie-Louise Legg, Ph.D., for enabling services; Miss Anna Clarke, BA, Barrister-at-Law, Commissioner for Oaths, etc., *(Whom God Preserve)*; Dr K. E. K. Rowson, MA, MD (Cantab.), Ph.D. (London), Dip.Bact.; Mrs E. J. Rowson, SRN, SCM; Master Frederick Rowson; Miss Rose Rowson; Sir Thomas Legg, KCB, QC; Dr R. A. Buttimore, MA, Ph.D.; Russell Clarke, Esq.; Miss Jan Dalley, Editrix and belle-lettrist *de nos jours*; Mr Kenneth Monkman, Squire of Coxwold; Professor Peter de Voogt *of Utrecht*; Mr Giles Gordon, FRSL; Captain Shaun Whiteside, RN; Dame Georgina Morley; Ian Thompson, MA; Dr David Zeitlyn, Ph. D., Lecturer in Social Anthropology at Stevanga, etc.; Kevin Jackson, Esq.; Thomas Lubbock, Esq.; Lord Mark Seddon, KGB and bar; William Self, Esq., Hierophant of ye Westway; Dr Eric Griffiths, SJ; Dr Blake Morrison; Lord Francis Wheen, Viscount Pleshey and with the humblest apologies my poor spirit will allow, Monsignor John Walsh.

I am, an' please your worships,

THE AUTHOR

THE
LIFE
AND
OPINIONS
OF
TRISTRAM SHANDY,
GENTLEMAN.

Ταρασσει τοὺς Ἀνθρώπους οὐ τὰ Πράγματα,
αλλα τὰ περι τῶν Πραγμάτων, Δογματα.

1996

The *minutest philosophers* show us incontestably, that the HOMUNCULUS is *created* by the *same* hand & endowed with the *same locomotive powers* and *faculties* with us:— That he *consists*, as we do, of *skin, hair, fat, flesh, veins, arteries, ligaments, nerves, cartileges, bones, marrow, brains, glands,* GENITALS, *humours and articulations* — and, in all senses of the word, is as *much* and as *truly* our *fellow-creature* as my LORD CHANCELLOR of ENGLAND.—

(*Marry,* my LORDS, *surely 'tis* FUNDAMENTALLY a *Treatise on* UNDERSTANDING!)

An' please Your Worships!

Nature never makes excellent things for mean or no uses!

He may be *benefited,* he may be *injured,* — he may *obtain redress;* — in a word, he has all the *claims* and *rights* of *humanity* which TULLY, PUFFENDORFF, *or the best ethic writers* allow to arise out of that *state* and *relation...*

For the *curious* and *inquisitive*, my BEGETTING was betwixt the *1st* SUNDAY & *1st* MONDAY in March *1718* — SHUT THE DOOR!

This date is *certain*, as my FATHER, you must *know*, was one of the *most regular* men in *everything* he did THAT EVER LIVED. As a *small* specimen of this EXTREME EXACTNESS of his — he had made it a *rule* for many years of his life, on the 1ST SUNDAY of every month throughout the year, to wind up a large CLOCK...

GRRRRRR-CLONK! GRRRRRR-CLONKK!

UHHNN! UHHHNN!

"Now, he had *likewise* gradually brought some other little FAMILY CONCERNMENTS to the *same* PERIOD in order, as he would often tell my UNCLE TOBY, to GET THEM OUT of the WAY at ONE TIME & be no more PLAGUED with them the *rest* of the month...

Well then, Brother Toby, I must to BED to discharge my MARITAL DUTIES...

A *consequence* of this was a *strange combination* of IDEAS in my MOTHER's MIND so that she could *never hear* the said CLOCK WOUND UP — but the thoughts of some OTHER THINGS unavoidably popped into her HEAD...

GRRRRRRR-CLONK! GRRRRRRRRR-CLONK!

UHHNN! UHHHNN!

And *vice versa*."

Pray, my dear, the CLOCK!

UHHNN! UHHNNNN!! WHAT?!??

Thus, on the 5th Day of *November* 1718, as near *9 months* as any HUSBAND could in *reason* expect — was *I* TRISTRAM SHANDY, Gentleman, brought forth into this SCURVY & DISASTROUS WORLD of ours.— I wish I had been born in the *Moon*, or in any of the PLANETS...

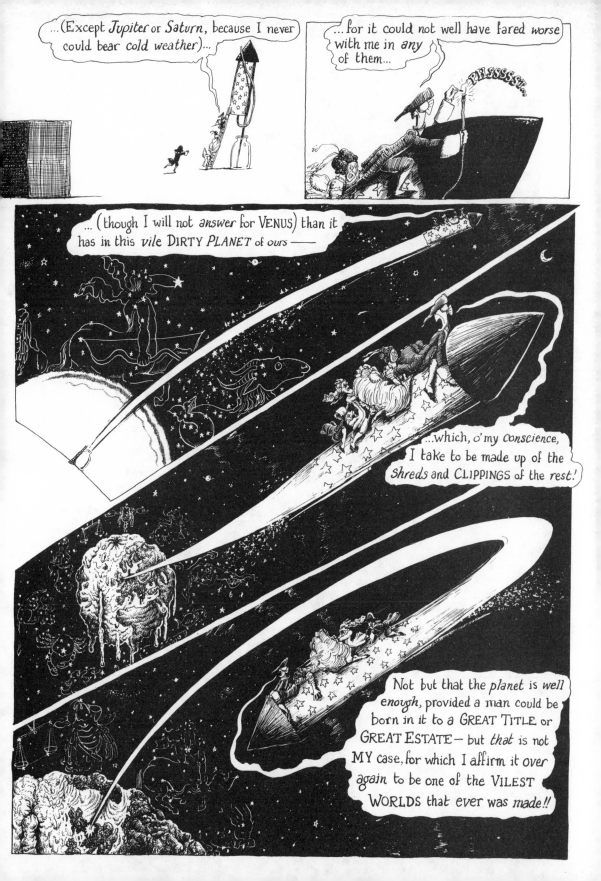

(AHEM!) In the *same village* where my father & mother dwelt, dwelt also a *thin, upright* MOTHERLY good old body of a *midwife* who had acquired no small degree of *reputation in* the WORLD; — by which *word* I would be understood, *your worships,* to mean *no more* of it than a *small circle* described upon the *greater circle* of the GREAT WORLD, of 4 *English miles diameter,* or thereabouts, of which the *good old woman's* cottage is supposed to be THE CENTRE...

4 miles

ZZZZZZ

Now, it came into the head of the *wife of the parson* of the parish that, inasmuch as there was *no such thing* as a MIDWIFE of any kind to be got at within less than SIX or SEVEN long MILES *riding* — it would be a *kindness* to the *whole parish,* & to the *poor creature herself,* to get her a *little instructed* in some of the *plain principles* of the business in order to set her up in it...

The parson joined his interest with his wife's in the *whole affair,* and in order to do things as they *should be,* and give the poor soul as good a title by *law* to practice — he cheerfully *paid* the fees for the ordinary licence *himself* (to the sum of *18s. 4d.*)...

...so that, betwixt them both, the good woman was *fully invested* in the *real & corporal* possession of her office, together with all its *rights, members & appurtenances* WHATSOEVER...

ORDINARY LICENCE of Midwifery

Spare Punctuation

7 miles

Dedication

My Lord,

I maintain this to be a dedication, notwithstanding its singularity in the three great essentials of matter, form and place: I beg, therefore, you will accept it as such, and that you will permit me to lay it, with the most respectful humility, at your Lordship's feet, — when you are upon them, — which you can be when you please; — and that is, my Lord, whenever there is occasion for it, and I will add, to the best purposes too. I have the honour to be,

My Lord,
Your Lordship's most obedient,
and most devoted,
and most humble servant,

TRISTRAM SHANDY

I solemnly declare to *all mankind*, that the above dedication was made for no one PRINCE, PRELATE, POPE or POTENTATE — *Duke, Marquis, Earl, Viscount* or *Baron*, of *this* or *any other* realm in *CHRISTENDOM!* I labour this point so particularly, merely to remove any offence which might arise against it, from the *manner* in which I *propose* to make the *most* of it; — which is the PUTTING IT UP fairly for PUBLIC SALE; which I *now do*. It is at any of your Lordships' service for

50 GUINEAS (which I am positive is 20 *GUINEAS* less than it ought to be afforded for, by any man of genius).

WHAT THE?!?

I Humbly dedicate this work to my BELOVED PUBLISHER for the invaluable help and support provided by his beautiful ACCOUNTS DEPARTMENT...

The fact of it *was*, he had been for *many* years lending his *good mount* (there was *none better* in the parish) close once a week to reach the *nearest MIDWIFE* — living 7 miles distant across vile country — making a *disproportionate* claim on his *other* expences (he needsmust purchase a new, good horse each 9 or 10 months), and conferring all his *charity* towards the *parish* to the *child-bearing* and-*getting* part, leaving *nothing* for the *impotent*, the *aged*, the *poor, sick* or *afflicted* — he resolved thus to ride the *last* poor nag (such as they had *made* him) to the *very end* of the chapter...

SO WHAT'S ALL THIS BIT ABOUT, EH?

HIST, MY POOCH!

PHUT PHUT PHUT!

An' please yer worship, we'm just nippin' over to the old biddy yonder!

The WORLD, no sooner had he bestirred himself on behalf of the *midwife* & her *licence*, judged — through *ignorance* or *malice* — a *cozening* pride in the parson's *act of* CHARITY — "that he would be *well mounted* once more and, if 'twere so, would *pocket* the expence of the *licence* TENFOLD the very 1st year — so that everybody was left to *judge* what were the parson's *motives* in the affair."

We'm named 'im after yer 'onour!

Gadzooks! My HORSE!

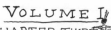

It is *high time* I introduced the MIDWIFE to you for GOOD & ALL — her *fame*, I must tell you, had spread itself to the very *out-edge* or CIRCUMFERENCE of that CIRCLE OF IMPORTANCE which, if I *remember*, I fixed at 4 or 5 miles from the smoke of her own chimney...

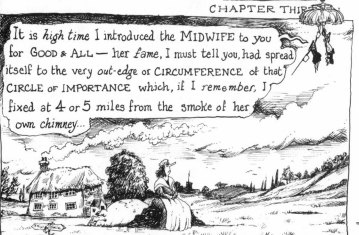

(I will include a MAP at the end of the *20th Volume*.) Meanwhile, we have various...

Accounts to reconcile & Anecdotes to pick up:

Inscriptions to make out & Stories to weave in:

Traditions to sift:

KING o' THE SHANDIES

Personages to call upon:

PROFESSOR DUMPENDEBAT MASTER OF POX CHIRURGEON OF NOSES

Panegyrics to paste up at *this* door: Pasquinades at *that*:

There is no END to it! And I am not yet BORN:— I have just been able, and that's all, to tell you *when* it happened, but not HOW;— so you see the thing is yet far from being accomplished. Come...

CHAPTER FIFTEEN

Whoever it was, my Uncle Toby's was a *character* that would have done *honour* to our *atmosphere*, had he not clearly derived his SINGULARITY more from BLOOD than either *wind* or *water*, for all the SHANDY FAMILY were of an *original* character — I mean the *males* — the *females* had *no* character at all —

Except, in'deed, my great AUNT DINAH, who about 60 years ago, was *married* & GOT WITH CHILD by the COACHMAN (for which my *father*, according to his *hypothesis* of *Christian names*, would often say, she might thank her *godfathers* & *godmothers*).

Bleat!

Bleat

Baaaaaa!

Now, my uncle TOBY SHANDY, Madam, was a gentleman with a *most extreme* & *unparalleled* MODESTY of NATURE, — though I may not *prejudge* whether this MODESTY of his was *NATURAL* or *ACQUIRED*...

OLD DAN BOREAS

Whichever way my Uncle came by it, 'twas nevertheless MODESTY in the *truest sense*, almost equalling even the MODESTY of a *WOMAN* in that FEMALE NICETY & inward *cleanliness* of MIND & FANCY so that he could never *bear* to hear the affair of my AUNT DINAH *touched* upon but with the greatest emotion...

A priori, had our Aunt DINAH been baptized SARAH JANE or even FANNY, I contend she would *not* have ENDED UP ROGERED by the COACHMAN!

For God's sake, and for MY sake, and for ALL our sakes, my dear brother SHANDY,—do let this story of our aunt's and her ASHES SLEEP IN PEACE;—how CAN you have so LITTLE FEELING & COMPASSION for the CHARACTER of our FAMILY?!?

Hrumph?

BAH! What is the character of a FAMILY to a HYPOTHESIS? Nay, if you come to that, what is the LIFE of a family?

The LIFE of a family?

Yes, the LIFE! How many 1000s of 'em are there EVERY YEAR that come CAST AWAY (in all civilized countries, at least)—and are considered as NOTHING but COMMON AIR in competition to an HYPOTHESIS?

In my plain sense of things, every such instance is downright MURDER, let who will commit it!

Ah ha! THERE lies your MISTAKE!

—for, in Foro Scientiae, there is no such thing as MURDER,—'tis only DEATH, brother!

At this my Uncle Toby would give vent to his passions in the usual channel when anything especially absurd was offered to him, by whistling half a dozen bars of "LILLABULLERO."

Now, I have a very strong PROPENSITY in me to continue very NONSENSICALLY. (Tee Hee!)

CONCLUSION OF YE FIRST
VOLUME

ALRIGHT, SO WHERE ARE WE NOW?

AH, MON CHERI, WE ARE IN THE LIMBO BETWEEN VOLUMES, A QUASI-PLATONIC PURGATORY OF INCOMPREHENSION, AWAITING SALVATION THROUGH THE INTERCESSION OF LITERARY CRITICS, EGAD!

AND LOOK, PETE! HERE COME SOME WILLING EXEGETES NOW! A MERRY TROUPE OF **LEAPING FRENCH DECONSTRUCTIONISTS!**

ALLEZ-OOOP!!

TOBIAS SHANDY *tribvnvs militv*
obsess

Once home, he was 4 years totally confined — suffering unspeakable miseries owing to a succession of exfoliations from the *os pubis* and the *os illium* upon the *coxendix* — in the very best apartment of my father's London house...

A. Tower
B. Tower-guard
C. Talus
D. Terreplein
E. Scrote-guard
F. Bastion & Counterfort
G. Scarp
H. Fossé
I. Cuvette (when dry)
J. Covered way
K. Counterscarp

Now, the HISTORY of a SOLDIER'S WOUND beguiles the pain of it, & my father encouraged his *friends & acquaintances* to chat an hour beside his brother Toby's *bedside*, the discourse frequently turning to the WOUND — & thence to the SIEGE *itself*.

L. Bastion of Demi-Lune
M. Pubeguarde
N. Fosse
O. Counterscarp
P. Covered Way
Q. Sally Port
R. Parapet
S. Glacis
T. Mound of Ravelin

However, these *conversations* brought my uncle Toby into some *unforeseen perplexities*. These arose out of the almost *insurmountable difficulties* he found in *telling* his story INTELLIGIBL when seeking to *pinpoint* the exact spot where he received the WOUND upon his GROIN — in giving such *clear distinctions* between the scarp & *counterscarp*, — the glacis & the COVERED WAY, — the HALF-MOON & the ravelin — the surrounding ground being also *cut & cross-cut* with a multitude of *dykes, drains, rivulets & sluices* on all sides —

SPLOSH!

A. Tower
R. Parapet
S. Glacis
E. Dyke
H. Fossé
O. Counterscarp
L. Half-Moons
E. Dyke

—as to make his company fully *comprehend* WHERE & WHAT he was *about*.

Then, Sir, as I am to understand it correctly, you were wounded up your COVERED WAY with a GLASS JAVELIN whilst climbing a GROYNE illuminated by a HALF MOON, yes?

ZZZZZZ

URRRRRGHH...

"These *perplexities* retarded his cure greatly for some 3 months together—

— & would have *laid* him in his grave had he *not hit upon* an expedient to extricate himself *out of them*."

No no, Doctor! I mean the DEMI-LUNE before the 2ND TERREPLEIN...

Hush, Captain Shandy!

ZZZZZZ

Of course, I meant just beyond the CUVETTE in the *fosse* behind the scarp but before the Counterscarp, you see?

Which was to acquire a *large map* of the FORTIFICATIONS of the TOWN & CITADEL of NAMUR so that he could *stick* a PIN upon the *identical spot* — in one of the *traverses*, about 30 *toises* from the *returning angle* of the trench, opposite to the *salient angle* of the *demi-bastion* of St.Roch — where he was standing when the stone wounded him upon the GROIN.

the CITY of NAMUR with the CASTLE & FORTIFIKATIONS

PI NG!

So that *no one* can say I have not allowed OBADIAH *time enough* — poetically speaking — both to go & come ——— Although the *hypercritic*, measuring the *true* distance betwixt the RINGING of the bell & the *rap* at the parlour door which disturbed my father's *dissertation* — as being 2 MINUTES, 13 SECONDS & ⅗ths — may thus *insult me* for such a *breach* in the UNITY of TIME!

I would *remind* him that in *that time* I have brought my uncle Toby from NAMUR, across FLANDERS, to ENGLAND — had him *4 years* ill upon my hands — got him 200 miles down into YORKSHIRE — which *must* have prepared your imaginations for the entrance of DR. SLOP upon our stage ——

Υοτ θε φυκ?

POETRY

If my *hypercritic* is *intractable* over those 2 MINUTES & 13 SECONDS, then I will *acquaint* him that OBADIAH had not got above 3 SCORE YARDS from the *stable yard* —

Ζευς ου α Ρικε!

PETER

WACKO!

— before he met with DR. SLOP — who, apprised by my father a week before that my *mother* was at her *full* reckoning, was taking a ride to SHANDY HALL to see how *things went* — was waddling through the *dirtiest* part of a *dirty lane* — when OBADIAH & his coach horse should turn the corner —

DR. SLOP being a *PAPIST*, he CROSSED himself, Sir ✝ — Pugh! when he *should* have held on to his *pummel* —

SPLOSH!

Now, when DR. SLOP entered the *back parlour* immediately following his *MOMENTOUS* encounter with Obadiah, here was a fair opportunity for my uncle Toby to have triumphed over my *father*, for no mortal could *dissent* from the opinion "That mayhap his sister might not care to let such a DR. SLOP come so near her *✳✳✳✳*" ——

Instead, the ring of the *bell* & the rap on the parlour door excited a very different train of thoughts; —— the 2 irreconcileable *pulsations* instantly brought STEVINUS, the great *engineer*, instantly into my uncle Toby's mind: ——

so that, once the doctor & OBADIAH had told their tales; —— my father had stepped upstairs to see my *mother*; —— the DOCTOR had been *washed* — *rubbed down* — *condoled with* — *felicitated* — got into a pair of OBADIAH's *pumps*; —— DR. SLOP had *remembered* that he had *left* his instruments — his *tire tête,* — his *new invented forceps,* — his *crotchet* — his SQUIRT *BEHIND HIM,* in a *green bays bag,* betwixt 2 *pistols,* at his bed's head! (RING! — CALL! — OBADIAH was sent back upon the COACH HORSE to fetch them) —— my father, my uncle Toby & DR. SLOP all 3 sat down to the fire together, & my uncle TOBY began to speak...

Your sudden & unexpected *ARRIVAL* instantly brought the great STEVINUS into my head, who, you must know, is a *favourite author* with me ——

Then I will lay 20 GUINEAS to a single crown piece that this SAME STEVINUS was an *ENGINEER* who has wrote *DIRECTLY upon* the SCIENCE of FORTIFICATION ——

BUZZ BUZZ BUZZ

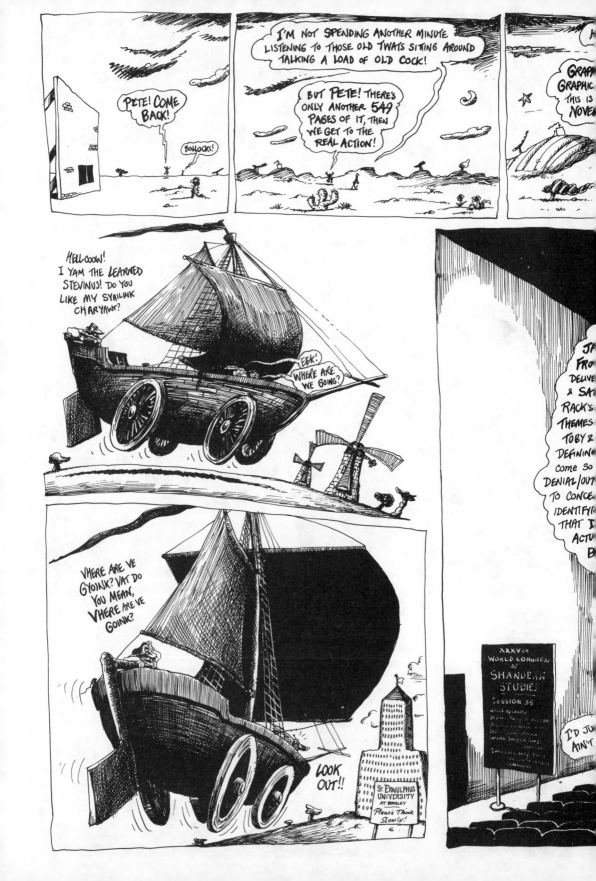

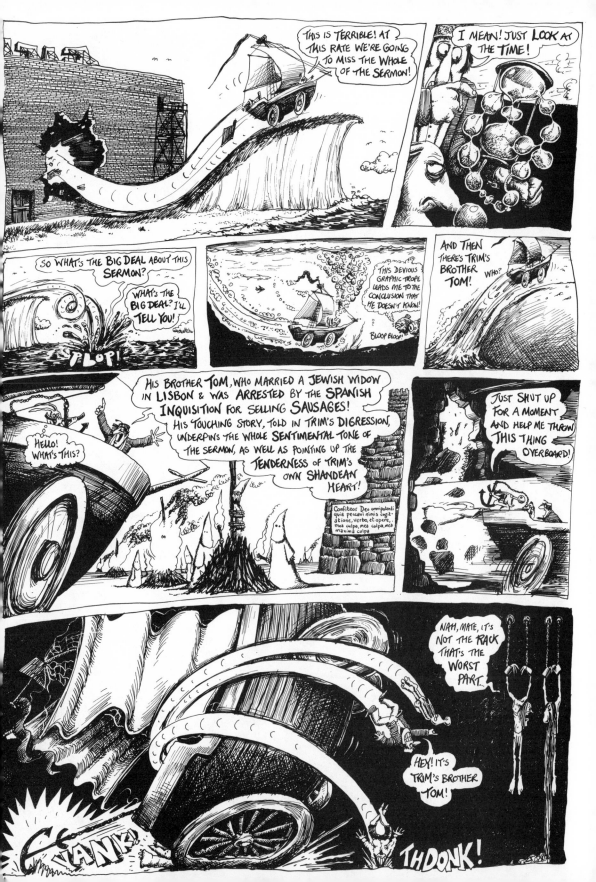

Amongst the many & excellent reasons, with which my *father* had urged my *mother* to accept DR. SLOP's assistance preferably to that of the *old woman*, — there was *one* of a very *singular* nature, which was —— That every man's WIT must come from every man's OWN *SOUL*; — And that it therefore followed that the *great difference* between the MOST ACUTE & MOST OBTUSE *understanding* arose from the *lucky* or *unlucky* organization of that *part* of the BODY where the SOUL principally took up her *residence* —————— My father therefore made the *subject* of his inquiry the IDENTICAL PLACE where the *SOUL* resides, whether it be *upon* the *top* of the PINEAL GLAND where DES CARTES had *fixed* it; ——————

—————————— or rather somewhere about the MEDULLA OBLONGATA, wherein it was generally agreed by Dutch Anatomists, that all the *minute* nerves from all the organs of the **7** senses CONCENTERED, like *streets* & *winding* alleys, into a SQUARE...

My father at first agreed with DES CARTES, until my uncle Toby told him of a *Walloon* officer at the Battle of Landen, who had *1 part* of his BRAIN *SHOT AWAY* by a *musket ball* — and another part TAKEN OUT after by a French surgeon; — & , after *all*, recovered , & did his duty *VERY WELL WITHOUT IT* —

If DEATH, reasoned my father, is nothing but the *separation* of the SOUL from the BODY; — & if it is *true* that people can do their business WITHOUT brains, — then *certes* the SOUL does *not* inhabit there. Q.E.D.

Fixing, then, on the SOUL residing within the MEDULLA in the CEREBELLUM, he struck upon the entirely SHANDEAN hypothesis, that the SUBTLETY & FINENESS of the Soul depended on the FINENESS of the *Network & Texture* of the CEREBELLUM *ITSELF.*

Thus he maintained...

SQUELCH!

But how great was his apprehension when he *further* understood that this *force* not only *injured* the BRAIN itself or *cerebrum* — but that it *necessarily* SQUEEZED & PROPELLED the *cerebrum* towards the *cerebellum*, which was the IMMEDIATE SEAT OF UNDERSTANDING!

But, if a child was turned TOPSY-TURVY — which was easy for an operator to do, & was extracted by the FEET; — then the CEREBELLUM was propelled towards the CEREBRUM, where it could do *no manner* of hurt.

BY HEAVENS! The World is in a conspiracy to drive out what LITTLE WIT God has given us! — & the professors of the obstetric art are listed into the SAME CONSPIRACY! What is it to ME which end of my SON comes foremost into the WORLD, provided all goes right after, & his CEREBELLUM escapes UNCRUSHED?

There was scarce a phenomenon of STUPIDITY or of GENIUS which he could not *readily solve* by this HYPOTHESIS, including why my brother BOBBY, coming into the world FOREMOST, turned out afterwards a lad of *wonderful slow parts* ——— and thus, as he had *failed* at ONE END, ——— he was determined to try the OTHER...

For G—d's sake, Bobby! What are you about NOW?!?

Assistance in achieving this end was not to be expected from one of the SISTERHOOD, who are not easily to be put out of their way, — and was therefore one of my father's *great reasons* in favour of a MAN OF SCIENCE over the OLD MIDWIFE, & DR. SLOP was the *fittest man* in *all the world* for my father's purpose; — for though Dr Slop's new invented FORCEPS was, he maintained, the safest instrument of deliverance, — yet, it seems, he had scattered a *word* or 2 in his book, in favour of EXTRACTION BY THE FEET — though *not* with a view to the SOUL'S good, as was my FATHER'S SYSTEM, — but for reasons *merely obstetrical* ——

This —

will account —

— for the *coalition* betwixt my father & DR. SLOP, in the *ensuing discourse*, which went a *little hard* against my UNCLE TOBY. But you will be *content* to wait for a *full explanation* of this — and how my uncle Toby got his MODESTY by the WOUND upon his GROIN, — and how I *lost* my NOSE by MARRIAGE ARTICLES — & how I should have the *misfortune* to be called TRISTRAM in *opposition* to my father's hypothesis, & the wish of the *whole family* ——

The Life and Opinions of
TRISTRAM SHANDY
Gentleman

Mvltitudinis imperitae non formido judicia; meis
tamen, rogo, parcant opvsculis——in quibis fvit
Propositi semper, a jocis ad seria, a seriis vicissim
ad jocos transire.

— JoAN. SARESBERIENSIS, Episcopus.
Lugdun.

Stevinus's
Fabled
Translating
Engine

I do not fear the opinions of the ignorant
crowd; yet I ask them to spare my
little work, in which it has always
been my purpose to pass from the
gay to the serious and from the serious
to the day. —— John of Salisbury
Policraticus

VOLUME III
Chapter One

I WISH, Dr. Slop, you had seen what prodigious armies we had in Flanders.

—What prodigious armies you had in Flanders!! Brother Toby...

GNNNNNNNN...

"By the authority of God Almighty, the Father, Son & Holy Ghost, & of the holy canons, & of the undefiled Virgin Mary, mother & patroness of our Saviour."

I think there is no necessity to read it aloud — I may as well read it to myself —

That's contrary to our treaty — besides, there is something so WHIMSICAL, especially in the latter part of it, I should grieve to lose the pleasure of your reading it.

"By the authority of God Almighty, the Father, Son & Holy Ghost, & of the undefiled Virgin Mary, mother & patroness of our Saviour, and of all the celestial virtues, angels, archangels, thrones, dominions, powers, cherubins & seraphins, & of all the holy patriarchs, prophets, & of all the apostles & evangelists, and of the HOLY INNOCENTS, who in the sight of the HOLY LAMB, are found worthy to sing the new song of the holy martyrs & holy confessors, & of the holy virgins, & of all the saints together, with the holy & elect of God —— May he (OBADIAH) BE DAMNED (for tying these KNOTS.) —— We excommunicate, & anathematize him, & from the thresholds of the HOLY CHURCH of GOD ALMIGHTY we sequester him, that he may be tormented, DISPOSED, & delivered over with Dathan & Abiram, & with those who say unto the Lord God, DEPART from us, we desire NONE of thy ways. And as fire is quenched with water, so let the LIGHT of him be put out for EVERMORE, unless it shall repent him (OBADIAH, OF THE KNOTS WHICH HE HAS TIED) and make satisfaction (for them.) AMEN.

May the FATHER who created man, CURSE HIM. —— May the SON who suffered for us, CURSE HIM. —— May the HOLY GHOST who was given to us in baptism, CURSE HIM (OBADIAH). —— May the HOLY CROSS which Christ for our salvation triumphing over his enemies, ascended, CURSE HIM. —— May the HOLY & ETERNAL VIRGIN MARY, mother of GOD, CURSE HIM. —— May all the ANGELS & ARCHANGELS, PRINCIPALITIES & POWERS, & all the HEAVENLY ARMIES, CURSE HIM.

Our armies swore terribly in Flanders, but nothing to this! For my own part, I could not have a heart to curse a DOG so.

May ST. JOHN the PRAE-CURSOR, & ST. JOHN the BAPTIST, & ST. PETER & ST. PAUL, & ST. ANDREW, & all other CHRIST's APOSTLES, together CURSE HIM. And may the rest of his DISCIPLES & FOUR EVANGELISTS, who by their preaching converted the UNIVERSAL WORLD, and may the holy & wonderful company of MARTYRS & CONFESSORS who by their HOLY WORKS are found pleasing to GOD ALMIGHTY, CURSE HIM. (OBADIAH)

May the HOLY CHOIR of the HOLY VIRGINS, who for the honour of CHRIST have despised the things of the world, **DAMN HIM.** —— May all the saints who from the BEGINNING of the WORLD to everlasting ages are found to be BELOVED of GOD, **DAMN HIM** —— May the heavens and earth, and all the HOLY THINGS remaining therein, **DAMN HIM** (OBADIAH) or her (or whoever ELSE had a hand in TYING THESE KNOTS)

May he (OBADIAH) be **DAMNED** wherever he be —— whether in the house or the stables, the garden or the field, or the highway, or in the path, or in the wood, or in the water, or in the church.—— May he be **CURSED** in LIVING, in DYING. ——————— May he be **CURSED** in EATING & DRINKING, in being hungry, in being thirsty, in fasting, in sleeping, in slumbering, in walking, in standing, in sitting, in lying, in working, in resting, in PISSING, in SHITTING, & in BLOODLETTING!

May he (OBADIAH) be cursed in all the faculties of his body.

May he be cursed INWARDLY & OUTWARDLY.—— May he be cursed in the hair of his head.
May he be cursed in his brains, & in his VERTEX,

That is a sad curse.

in his temples, in his forehead, in his ears, in his EYE-BROWS, in his CHEEKS, in his jaw-bones, in his NOSTRILS, in his fore-teeth & grinders, in his lips, in his throat, in his shoulders, in his wrists, in his arms, in his hands, in his fingers.

May he be **DAMNED** in his mouth, in his breast, in his heart & purtenance, down to the VERY STOMACH.

May he be **CURSED** in his REINS, & in his GROIN, God in heaven forbid! in his thighs, in his genitals and in his hips, and in his knees, his legs, his feet, & TOE-NAILS.

May he be **CURSED** in all the joints & articulations of his MEMBERS, from the top of his head to the soal of his foot, may there be no soundness in him.

May the SON of THE LIVING GOD, with all the glory of HIS MAJESTY, **CURSE HIM**, & may HEAVEN, with all the POWERS which move therein, rise up against him, CURSE & DAMN HIM (Obadiah) unless he repent & MAKE SATISFACTION.

Amen. So be *it*, —so be it. Amen.

It would not be a CHERRY-STONE the WORSE. I maintain it, it would have broke the CEREBELLUM (unless indeed the skull had been as HARD as a GRANADO) & turned it all into a PERFECT POSSET!

Pshaw! a child's head is naturally as soft as the PAP of an APPLE — and besides, I could have extracted by the feet after.

Not you

I rather wish you would **begin** that way.

Pray do!

And pray, good woman, after all, will you take upon you to say it may not be the child's HIP, as well as the child's HEAD?

'Tis certainly the HEAD.

Because, as positive as these old ladies generally are, — 'tis a point very difficult to know, — and yet of the greatest conse-quence to be known — because, Sir, if the HIP is mistaken for the HEAD — there is a possibility (if it is a BOY) that the FORCEPS ——

* *

There is no such danger with the HEAD.

No, in truth, but when your possibility has taken place at the HIP — you may as well take off the HEAD TOO...

'Tis owing to this that in our computations of TIME, we are so used to MINUTES, HOURS, WEEKS & MONTHS,—& of CLOCKS (I wish there was not a CLOCK in the KINGDOM) to measure out their several portions to us, & to those who belong to us,—that 'twill be well, if in time to come, THE SUCCESSION OF OUR IDEAS be of any use or service to us at all. Now, whether we observe it or no, in every sound man's head, there is a regular succession of ideas of one sort or other, which follow each other in train just like ——

A train of artillery?

A train of a FIDDLESTICK! — which follow & succeed one another in our minds at certain distances, just like the images in the inside of a LANTHORN turned round by the heat of a candle. ——

I declare mine are more like a SMOAK—JACK.

Then, brother Toby, I have nothing more to say to you upon the subject.

PHWUMP!

— until we get into the *very heart* of Russian & Asiatic *Tartary.*

Now, throughout this *long tour* which I have led you, you observe the *good people* are *far* better off than in the *polar countries* we have just left: for if you hold your *hand* over your eyes you may perceive some small *glimmering* of WIT, with a *considerable provision* of good plain *household* JUDGMENT, in the *proper balance* the best to put them to *USE.*

Now, Sir, —

if I conduct you *home* again —

—into this *warmer & more luxuriant* ISLAND — where we have more *ambition, & pride, & envy, & lechery,* & other *whoreson* passions upon our *hands* to subject to *reason,* —— it must be *confessed* that, as our AIR blows *hot & cold,* — wet & dry *10 times a day,* we have WIT & JUDGMENT in *no regular* or *settled* way; —

— so that *sometimes* for NEAR 50 YEARS together there is very little WIT *or* JUDGMENT, either to be *seen* or *heard* of amongst us —

— then *all* of a sudden they shall BREAK OUT & take a fit of running again like *fury* & we drive all the WORLD before us, —————

A STATESMAN turning the political wheel against the stream of corruption instead of *with it.*

A BROTHER of the FACULTY upon his knees in tears begging forgiveness of a *martyred victim;* — offering a fee, instead of *taking* one ————

A COALITION of the GOWN, driving a damned, dirty, vexatious cause *out* of the great doors, instead of *in;* ——

—rashly determining a litigated point in 5 & 20 *minutes,* which, with the cautious pros & cons required in so *intricate* a proceeding, might have taken up as *many months!* As for the *clergy* ———

No, 'tis safer to *draw a curtain across* —

—And *hasten* from it as *fast* as we can—

To the *main & principal point* I have undertaken to *clear up,* — & that is, how it comes to pass

—That your men of *least* WIT

— are reported to be men of *most* JUDGMENT.

Zounds! The Captain's DUTCH DRAWBRIDGE!

ZZZZZZZZZZZZZZZZZZZZZZZZZZZZZ

Skrunch!!!

Observe this *cane chair* I sit upon. See the 2 KNOBS on the top of the back of it.

ZZZZZZZZZZZZZZZZZZZZZZZZZZZZZZZZZZZZ

Clah Cla

Now, *here* stands WIT, & *there* stands JUDGMENT, close beside it — You see, they are the *highest* & most *ornamental* parts of its frame —— as WIT & JUDGMENT are of *OURS* —

Now, for the sake of an *experiment* — let us for a moment take off one of these 2 curious ornaments from the *pinnacle* of the chair —

Thdonk!!

Clomp!

Did you ever see in the whole course of your lives, such a ridiculous business as *this* has made of it? Why, 'tis as miserable a sight as a *dog with one ear*; & there is as much sense & symmetry in the one as in the other.

So it is with WIT & JUDGMENT, as proven by your *graver gentry*

Tush, you licentious scoundrel!

who, having little or *no chance* in aiming at JUDGMENT — unless they laid hold of WIT — by an effort of philosophy, could not be satisfied with what little WIT they *snatched up* & *secreted* under their *beards* & *periwigs*, without they raised a *hue* & *cry* against WIT's *LAWFUL OWNERS*.

Splodge

Parp

Poop

The cry was so *deep* & *solemn* a one, & what with the help of *great wigs, long beards, grave faces* & other implements of *deceit*, against the POOR WITS, that even the great *Locke* himself was deceived by it —— which, by the bye, is one of the *many* & *vile* impositions which GRAVITY & GRAVE folks have to answer for hereafter....

This is a MORAL OUTRAGE, you impudent rogue!

Parp!

ZZZZZZZ

ZZZZZZZZZZZZZZZ ZZZZZZZZZZZZZZZZZZZZZZZZZZZZZZZZZZZZZZZZZ

Thrrrrrpppsstt

May it please your honour, they are 2 mortar pieces for a SEIGE next summer, which I have been making out of a pair of JACKBOOTS, which Obadiah told me your honour had left off wearing—

BY HEAVEN! I have not one appointment belonging to me which I set so much store by as I do those JACKBOOTS — they were our GREAT-GRANDFATHER's, Brother Toby — they were hereditary!

My DUTCH DRAWBRIDGE destroyed? Gracious heavens!

I hate these perpetuities — but these JACKBOOTS have been in the family since the Civil Wars — Sir Roger Shandy wore them at the Battle of Marston Moor!

I'll pay you for them, brother Shandy — I'll pay £10 this moment!

Well, all is quiet & hush at last above stairs —— I hear not 1 foot stirring. Prithee, Trim, who is in the Kitchen?

There is no 1 soul in the kitchen except Dr. Slop...

CONFUSION! Not one SINGLE THING has gone right this day!

Had I faith in astrology, I would have sworn some RETROGRADE PLANET was hanging over this UNFORTUNATE HOUSE of mine, & turning every individual thing in it out of its place!

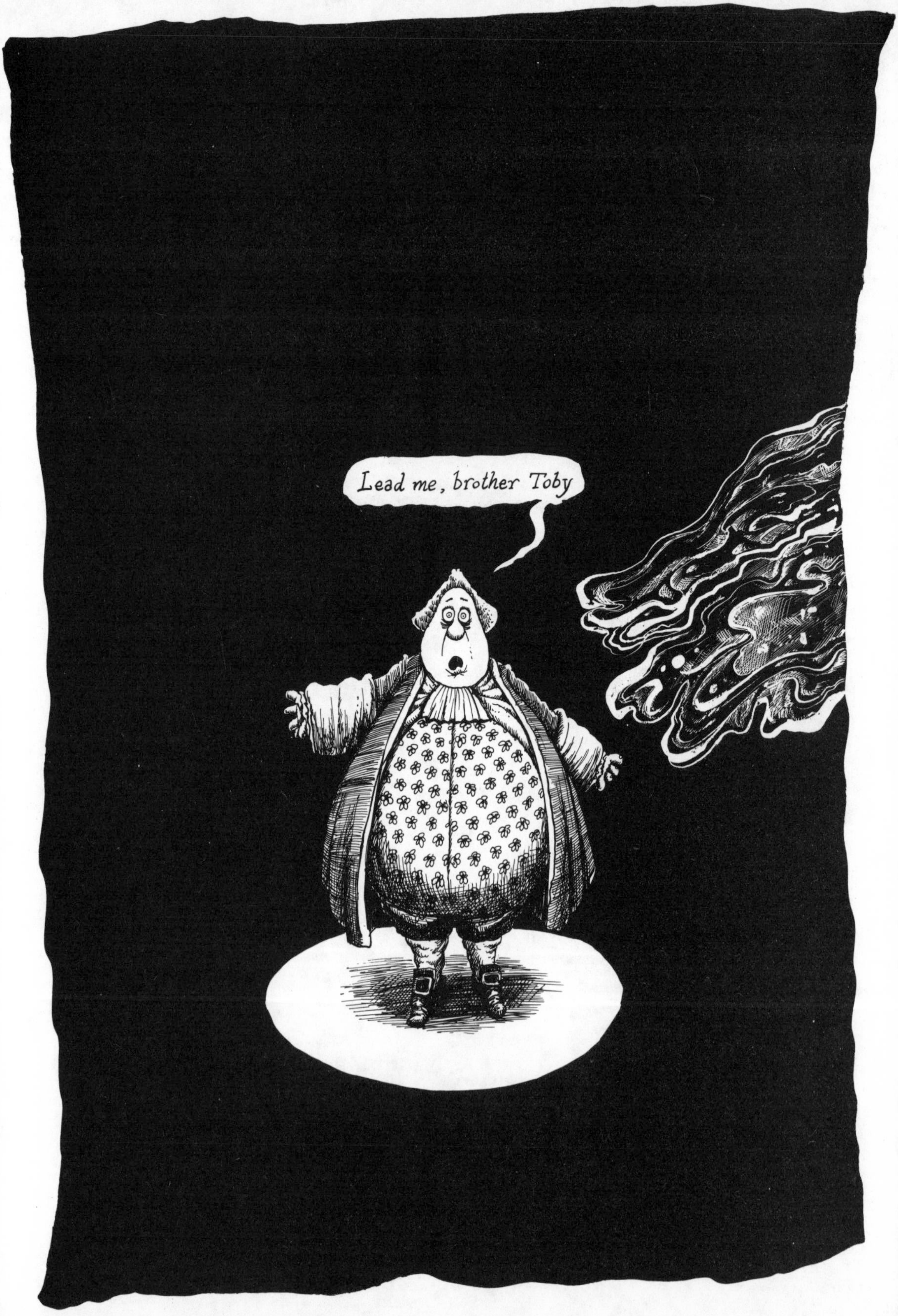
Lead me, brother Toby

Flopp!

that it lay him open to some of the *oddest & most whimsical* distresses, of which this particular one whick he sunk under at present is as *strong* an example as *can be given.*

No doubt the *breaking down* of the *bridge* of a *child's nose* by the edge of a pair of FORCEPS —— however scientifically applied —— would *vex* any man in the world who was at so much pains in begetting a child as was my *father* —— yet it will not account for the *extravagance* of his affliction, nor will it justify the *unchristian* manner he *abandoned & surrendered* himself to it ———

Gnnnnnnnnnnhvhhhnnnnnhhhnn

Now, as my *great-grandmother* outlived my *grandfather* by 12 years, my father was obliged to pay out the JOINTURE, to support my great-grandmother in her widowhood, of £150 half yearly (on *Michaelmas* & *Lady-day*) - during all that time ——

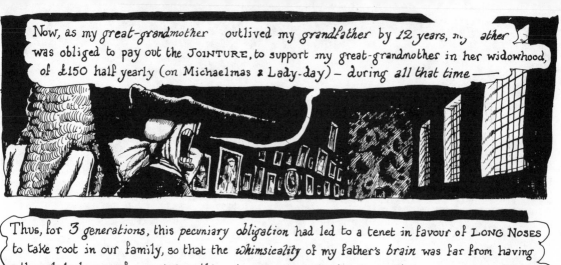

Thus, for 3 *generations*, this *pecuniary obligation* had led to a tenet in favour of LONG NOSES to take root in our family, so that the *whimsicality* of my father's *brain* was far from having the *whole honour* of conceiving this *strange notion*. He did his part, however, & would often declare that he did not conceive how the *greatest family in England* could stand it out against an *uninterrupted succession* of 6 or 7 SHORT NOSES ——

—— whereas the *same number* of LONG & JOLLY NOSES, following 1 another in a *direct line*, would *raise* & *hoist* it up into the BEST VACANCIES in the KINGDOM —— he would often *boast* that the Shandy family's fortunes since *King Harry the VIIIth's* time *never recovered the blow* of my GREAT-GRANDFATHER's NOSE ——

Now my father, once he had picked up his *opinions*, accordingly *held fast* by 'em, both with *teeth & claws* —— would fly to whatever he could lay his *hands* on ——

There was one *plaguy rub* in the way of this — the SCARCITY of MATERIALS; inasmuch as few men of *great genius* had exercised *their parts* in writing books upon the subject of great noses. So, though my father's library was *not great*, to make amends it was *curious*.

He had the great good fortune to set off well, in getting *Bruscambille's* prologue upon LONG NOSES; —— then *Prignitz* —— who, having examined above **4000** different skulls in upwards of **20** *charnel houses* in Silesia, maintained that the NOSE'S PROXIMITY to the force & warmth of the *imagination* —— blood & animal spirits being *impelled* into its ducts & sinuses —— the excellency of a NOSE is in *direct arithmetical proportion* to the excellency of the *wearer's fancy* ——

Then *Scroderus* — who disputed *Prignitz*, who affirmed that the *fancy* begat the *nose*, that on the contrary, — the *nose* begat the *fancy* —

To *this* was added *Bouchet's Evening Conferences* & *Ambrose Paraeus*, who was chief surgeon & *nose*-mender to Francis the Ninth of France —

SLAM!

— and stated that the *length* & *goodness* of the NOSE was owing simply to *either* the *softness* & *flaccidity* or the *firmness* & *elastic repulsion* of the NURSE's BREAST —

BOING!

(Parenthetically — my father struggled heartily & in vain to extract the *mystic significance* from the LEARNED ERASMUS's bald statement that a *long nose* is *not without its domestic conveniences*; for that in a case of *distress* — and for a want of a *pair of bellows*, it will do excellently well "to stir up the fire") —

PHFFFSSTTT!!

— and above all, he acquired the *great & learned* HAFEN SLAWKENBERGIUS ——————— O Slawkenbergius! thou faithful analyzer of my *Disgrázias*, ——— thou sad foreteller of so many of the whips & short turns which have come *slap* upon me from the shortness of my NOSE, & no *other* cause that I am conscious of ———————

Hafen Slawkenbergius, Sir, has taken in the *whole subject,* ——— examined *every part* of it DIALECTICALLY ——— then brought it into *full day* ——— collating, collecting & compiling all that had been wrote or wrangled thereupon in the schools & the porticos of the *learned*: so that Slawkenbergius *his book* may properly be considered not only as a *model* — but as a thorough-stitched DIGEST and regular *institute* of NOSES; comprehending in it all that is, or can be needful to be *known* about them.

But before I tell you the *9th tale* from SLAWKENBERGIUS's *10th decad* to display more exactly the *depth* of his POLYMATHY upon the full *universe* of NOSES, to avoid all confusion, it may not be amiss to explain *my own meaning* & DEFINE what I would *willingly* be understood to *mean* by the term NOSE: being of opinion, that in narratives of *strict morality* & *close reasoning* such as *this* I am engaged in —— the *neglect* of PRECISION & CLARITY of MEANING is INEXCUSABLE; and Heaven is *witness* how the world has *revenged itself* upon those who leave *too many* OPENINGS to equivocal strictures, —— depending *so much* as I have done, *all along*, upon the *cleanliness* of my readers' *imaginations*.

I define a nose *thus* —— entreating my auditors, both *male* & *female*, of what age, complexion, & condition soever, for the *love* of God & their own souls, to guard against the *temptations* & *suggestions* of the DEVIL & suffer him by no *art* or *wile* to put *any other* IDEAS into their *minds*, than what I put into my *own definition* —————— for by the word   NOSE, throughout all this *long discussion of noses*, & in every other *part* of my work the word *NOSE* occurs —————

Well hung Double Entendre

I declare, by that word I mean a NOSE, & nothing more, or less ——
Conclusion of Volume the Third

VOLUME IV
SLAWKENBERGIUS'S TALE

EDITOR'S NOTE

Following the Great Fire at Shandy Hall in 1837, it was believed that no trace of the 9th tale of the 10th decad of *Hafen Slawkenbergius de Nasis* remained, beyond a charred scrap of paper bearing the words "*se apud Nasorum promontorium fuisse, Francofurtum*". Thus countless generations of academic and general readers of the "Life & Opinions of Tristram Shandy" have suffered under the double burden of, first, having to read a version of the book with a gaping hole at the beginning of Volume IV, and secondly having to guess, with the meagrest of help from the rest of Tristram's text, what Slawkenbergius's 9th tale might *actually* be about.

Although it is now accepted that the actual text of the 9th tale is lost for ever, a discovery made in 1988 has enabled us to fill at least some of the gaps. Among the papers found in the library of Judge Stephen Yorick, latterly Her Majesty's Chief Inspector of Ears, Noses & Throats (which also famously contained over 35,000 different editions of *Tristram Shandy*) was a manuscript volume measuring about 6¾ x 4⅞ in (c. 170 x 125mm), bound in andalusianed goat velum, the gatherings separately stitched to stiff guards, foliated *dextra* but likewise exfoliated *sub-dextra*. The distinguishing mark *Slawk 31* is borne on the spine & flyleaf, anticled. A rouched refoliation is evidenced as the 1st leaf now bears the old number 198 in ink, struck out and replaced by 42 in crayon. The volume contains 5 illustrations from different editions or adaptations of Slawkenbergius's 9th tale. Using newly refined crypto-phrenological dating techniques developed at the Department of Epistemology at the University of Tashkent, V. I. Kantachurian & her team, in association with Professor Sir Julian Sykes-Wolsey at the Killane Memorial Centre for Vacancy at Stevenage, have gone some considerable way towards reconstructing the narrative of the 9th tale, thus filling one of the more enduring lacunae in English letters.

PLATE I

Anonymous German Woodcut for the popular vulgate edition of Slawkenbergius, printed by Hieronymous Schlefen, Basle, 1658.

A stranger arrives at the gate of Strasburg, announcing that he has recently visited the Promontary of NOSES, & is on his way to Frankfort but intends returning a month hence to Strasburg before travelling on to the borders of Crim Tartary.

The enormous size of the stranger's NOSE causes considerable controversy, dividing the town between those who believe to be a REAL NOSE & those who think it FALSE.

The intention by some of the citizens to *touch* the NOSE to settle the issue is greeted by the stranger to defend his nose with his *unsheathed* SCVMETAR.

PLATE II

Engraving by Albrecht Dürer from the so-called "Cardinal's" edition of *Hafen Slawkenbergivs de Nasis*, Dresden, 1518. Royal Collection.

The stranger embarks for Frankfort upon his mule, talking to himself of his love for the fair JULIA, from whom, for unspecified reasons, he is estranged.

PLATE III

Overleaf Engraving by William Hogarth, published separately 1735, with verse by Colley Cibber(?). Prints & Drawings Collection, British Museum.

In the stranger's absence Strasburg is left in tumult over the truth or falsity of his nose. A trumpeter's wife, having stolen her husband's horn, advertises her testimony as to the *truth* of the nose, while the *bandy-legged* drummer, who insists the nose is *false*, has his disquisition interrupted by the collapse of his husting.

Professors from the University, blind & guided by a nose-less syphilitic negro child holding a jar containing a monstrously-nosed foetus, rehearse the different sides of the argument. In the centre of the picture, Lutheran & Catholic Divines, respectively pro-& anti-Nosean, come to blows. Behind them, in an upper room, the Abbess of Quedlinburg swoons in her chambers while an urchin taunts her with a bucket of eels. In the town a mob attacks the Office of Noses. A mongrel cur chews the nose off a drunken, crippled beggar. Two figures in shadow use a nose-lengthening machine, a common attraction at 18th century street fairs.

Meanwhile, in his coach the French Ambassador observes all & smiles menacingly to himself.

Through STRASBURG's streets the CONS & PROS   As every Tom & Dick & Harry
In tumult fly around ye NOSE;   Debates ye NOSE's truth. Why,
The stranger gone, his snout's condition   Here the Priests, in righteous Ire
Is now the prey to SUPPOSITION   Defame ye NOSE 'gainst PASTO[r]

Invented, Design'd & Engrav'd by Wm. Hogarth & Publish'd According to Act of Parliament June ye 25. 1735.

say 'tis true; while Doctors blind
nize ye NOSE after its kind;
bbess swoons, nor relics' balm
ooth her or keep Strasburg calm;

The absent' stranger, astride his mule
Makes everyman a BEDLAM's FOOL
As arguments grow more intense
(The stranger's due a FORTNIGHT HENCE).

PLATE IV

Aubrey Beardsley, Ink on Paper, originally intended for the 6th issue of *The Yellow Book* but suppressed by Beauleduc, 1894. Private Collection.

Hastening to return to Strasburg, where the entire population eagerly awaits him, the stranger stops for the night at a wayside inn. There he meets a traveller who greets him as "Diego". The traveller is Fernandez, Diego's lover Julia's brother! Fernandez, as instructed by Julia, hands Diego a letter, which reads in part [according to the Tashkent CAT-scan]:-

"Seig. DIEGO.

Whether my suspicions of your nose were justly excited or not — 'tis not now to enquire — it is enough I have not had firmness to put them to further tryal...O my Diego! If the gentleness of your carriage has not belied your heart you will fly to me, almost as fast as you fled from me..."

Assured once more of Julia's love, Diego, with Fernandez, sets forth at once for Lyons, where Julia lies in expectation and some distress. Once reunited, all three cross the Pyrenean mountains and get safe to Valadolid, even as the Strasburgers set forth *en masse* to await Diego's return on the Frankfort Road.

PLATE V.

George Grosz. Artwork for a poster for Erwin Piscator's production of Bertolt Brecht's "Slawkenbergissimus". Berlin 1922. Private Collection.

The Strasburgers, still in tumultuous disagreement over the true nature of the Stranger's Nose, await his return one month after his arrival first sparked the controversy. The entire population of Strasburg congregates in feverish expectation outside the city walls on the Frankfort road, leaving Strasburg empty & unguarded. Thus abandoned, it falls easy victim to the invading armies of King Louis XIV of France pursuing the principles of Universal Monarchy, and so becomes not the first fortress in History lost by NOSES.

Heavens! How can this ever be translated into *good English?* —— There seems in some passages to want a *6th* sense to do it *rightly* —— What can Slawkenbergius *mean* by "the *lambent pupilability* of slow, low, dry chat, 5 notes below the *natural tone*"?

Madam, 'tis not worth *stooping* for...

I thank thee, Trim

I can never think of his & my poor brother Tom's MISFORTUNES (for we were all 3 school-fellows) but I cry like a coward—— to think of 2 virtuous lads with hearts as warm in their bodies, & as honest as God could make them—— & fall into SUCH EVILS! Poor Tom, to be tortured upon a rack for nothing but marrying a Jew's widow who sold SAUSAGES —— honest Dick Johnson's soul to be scourged out of his body, for the ducats another man put into his knapsack! O! These are misfortunes, may it please your honour, worth lying down & crying over!

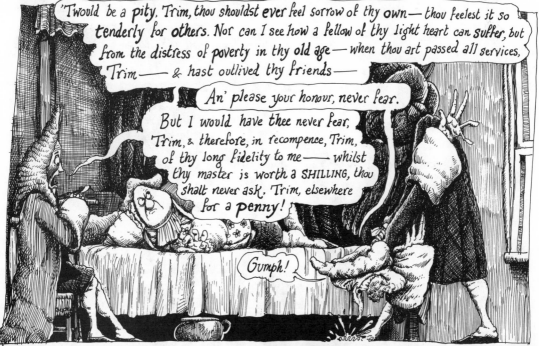

'Twould be a pity, Trim, thou shouldst ever feel sorrow of thy own—— thou feelest it so tenderly for others. Nor can I see how a fellow of thy light heart can suffer, but from the distress of poverty in thy old age—— when thou art passed all services, Trim—— & hast outlived thy friends——

An' please your honour, never fear.

But I would have thee never fear, Trim, & therefore, in recompence, Trim, of thy long fidelity to me—— whilst thy master is worth a SHILLING, thou shalt never ask, Trim, elsewhere for a penny!

Gumph!

I have left Trim my bowling-green!

I have left him, moreover, A PENSION.

When I reflect, brother Toby, upon MAN, & take a view of that dark side of him which represents his life as open to so many causes of trouble — when I consider, brother Toby, how of we eat the bread of affliction, & that we are born to it, as to the portion of our inheritance

I was born to nothing but my commission. Zooks! did not my uncle leave you 120 pounds a year? What could I have done without it?

That's another concern. But I say, Toby, though MAN is of all others the most curious vehicle

Yet at the same time is of so slight a frame, & so totteringly put together, that the sudden jerks & hard joltings it unavoidably meets with in this rugged journey, would overset it & tear it to pieces a dozen times a day — was it not, brother Toby, that there is a SECRET SPRING within us —

Which spring I take to be RELIGION.

WILL THAT SET MY CHILD'S NOSE ON?

It makes everything straight for us.

Figuratively speaking, dear Toby, it may, for aught I know, but the spring I am speaking of, is that great & elastic power within us of counterbalancing EVIL, which, like a secret spring in a well-ordered machine though it can't prevent the shock — at least it imposes upon our sense of it.

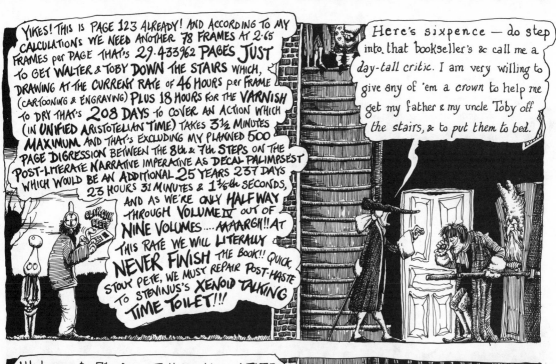
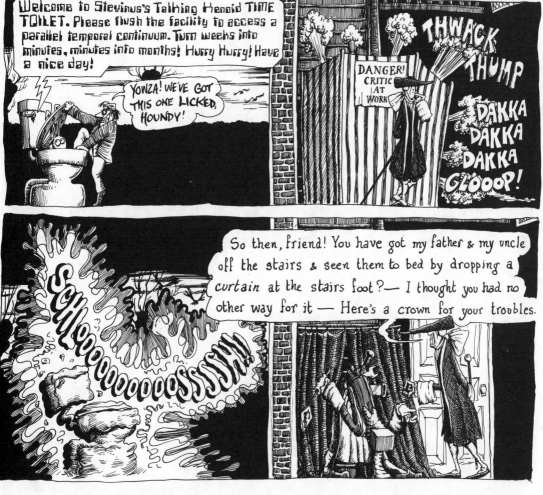

CHAPTER THIRTEEN

Then reach me my breeches off the chair— There's not a moment's time to dress you, sir—

—the child is as black in the face as my

As your, what?

Bless me, sir, the child's in a FIT!

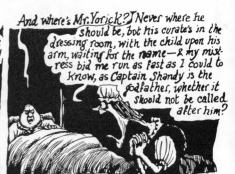

And where's Mr. Yorick? Never where he should be, but his curate's in the dressing room, with the child upon his arm, waiting for the name—& my mistress bid me run as fast as I could to know, as Captain Shandy is the godfather, whether it should not be called after him.

Were one sure that the child was expiring, one might as well compliment my brother Toby as not—& 'twould be a pity, in such a case, to throw away so great a name as TRISMEGISTUS upon him—But he may recover.

No, I'll get up.

There's no time, the child's as black as my shoe!

TRISMEGISTUS.

But stay—thou art a leaky vessel, Susannah: canst thou carry TRISMEGISTUS in thy head, the length of the gallery without scattering?

Can I?

If she can, I'll be shot.

SLAM

'Tis TRIS—something There is no Christian name in the world beginning with TRIS—but TRISTRAM.

Then 'tis TRISTRAM-GISTUS.

There is no GISTUS to it, noodle! 'tis my own name! TRISTRAM &c., &c., &c., &c.

She has not forgot the name?

No, no.

And how does your mistress?

As well as can be expected.

Pish!

CHAPTER FOURTEEN

If my wife will but venture him, brother Toby, TRISMEGISTUS shall be dressed & brought down to us, whilst you & I get our breakfasts together:——

Go, tell Susannah, Obadiah, to step here. She is run upstairs this very instant, sobbing & crying & wringing her hands as if her heart would break.——

We shall have a rare month of it; fire, water, women, wind—brother Toby, to have so many jarring elements breaking loose, & riding triumph in every corner of a gentleman's house

Little boots it to the peace of a family, brother Toby, that you & I possess ourselves, & sit here silent & unmoved—whilst such a storm is whistling over our heads——

And what's the matter, Susannah? They have called the child TRISTRAM—& my mistress is just got out of an hysteric fit about it—

No!

'tis not my fault! I told him it was TRISTRAM-GISTUS!

Make tea for yourself, brother Toby.

Go to the bowling-green for Corporal Trim.

CHAPTER FIFTEEN

Your honour has heard, I imagine, of this unlucky accident?

O yes Trim, & it gives me great concern.

But I hope your honour will do me the justice to believe it was not in the least owing to me—

To thee—Trim! 'twas Susannah & the curate's folly betwixt them

What business could they have together in the garden?

In the gallery thou meanest.

2 misfortunes are twice as many at least as are needful to be talked over at 1 time—the mischief done to the fortifications may be told his honour afterwards.

An' please your honour.

For my own part, Trim, though I can see little or no difference betwixt my nephew being called TRISTRAM or TRISMEGISTUS, yet the thing sits so near my brother's heart—

For he says there never was a great or heroic action performed since the world began by one called TRISTRAM.

'Tis all fancy, an' please your honour.

I fought just as well when the regiment called me TRIM, as when they called me James Butler!

And for my own part, had I been called ALEXANDER I could have done no more at Namur than my duty

Bless your honour!—does a man think of his Christian name when he goes upon the attack?

Or when he stands in the trench, Trim?

Or when he enters a breach?

Or forces the lines?

Or facing a platoon?

Or when he marches up the glacis?

CHAPTER SIXTEEN

MY FATHER'S LAMENTATION

It is in vain longer to struggle as I have done against this most uncomfortable of human persuasions — I see it plainly, that either for my own sins, brother Toby, or the sins & follies of the Shandy family, heaven has thought fit to draw forth the heaviest of its artillery against me; and that the prosperity of my child is the point upon which the whole force of it is directed to play —

Such a thing would batter the whole universe about our ears, brother Shandy, if it was so —

Unhappy Tristram! child of wrath! child of decrepitude! interruption! mistake! & discontent! What 1 misfortune or disaster in the book of embryotic evils, that Could unmechanize thy frame, or entangle thy filaments! which has not fallen upon thy head, or ever thou camest into the world! — what evils in thy passage into it! what evils since! — produced into being, in the decline of thy father's days, when the powers of his imagination & of his body were waxing feeble — when radical heat & radical moisture, the elements which should have tempered thine, were drying up; & nothing left to found thy stamina in, but negations — 'tis pitiful — brother Toby, at the best, & called out for all the little help that care & attention on both sides could give it. But how we were defeated! You know the event, brother Toby, 'tis too melancholy a one to be repeated now, — when the few animal spirits I was worth in the world, & with which memory, fancy & quick parts should have conveyed, — were all dispersed, confused, confounded, scattered, & sent to the devil.

Here then was the time to have put a stop to this persecution against him;——& tried an experiment at least——whether **calmness & serenity of mind** in your sister, with a due attention, brother Toby, to her evacuation & repletions——and the rest of her non-naturals, might not, in a course of **9 months'** gestation, have set all things to rights.——My child was **bereft of these!**——What a **teazing life** did she lead herself, and consequently her **foetus too**, with that nonsensical anxiety of hers about lying-in in town?

I thought my sister submitted with the **greatest patience**——I never heard her utter one **fretful word** about it——

She **fumed inwardly**; & that, let me tell you, brother, was **10 times worse** for the child——& then! what battles did she fight with me, & what **perpetual storms** about the midwife——

There she gave vent.

VENT!

But **what** was all this, my dear Toby, to the injuries done us by my child's coming **head foremost** into the world, when **all** I wished in this **general wreck** of his frame, was to have saved this little **casket unbroke, unrifled**——

With all my precaution, how was my system turned **topsy-turvy** in the womb with my child! his **head exposed** to the hand of violence, & a **pressure of 470** pounds averdupois weight acting so perpendicularly upon its **apex**——that at this hour 'tis 90 per cent. insurance, that the fine **net-work** of the intellectual web be not rent & torn to 1000 tatters.

——Still we could have done.——**Fool, coxcomb, puppy**——give him but a NOSE——Cripple, Dwarf, **Driveller, Goosecap**——(shape him as you will) the door of **Fortune** stands open——fate might have done her **worst.**

Still, brother Toby, there was one cast of the **die left** for our child after all——**O Tristram! Tristram! Tristram!**

We will send for Mr Yorick.

You may send for whom you will.

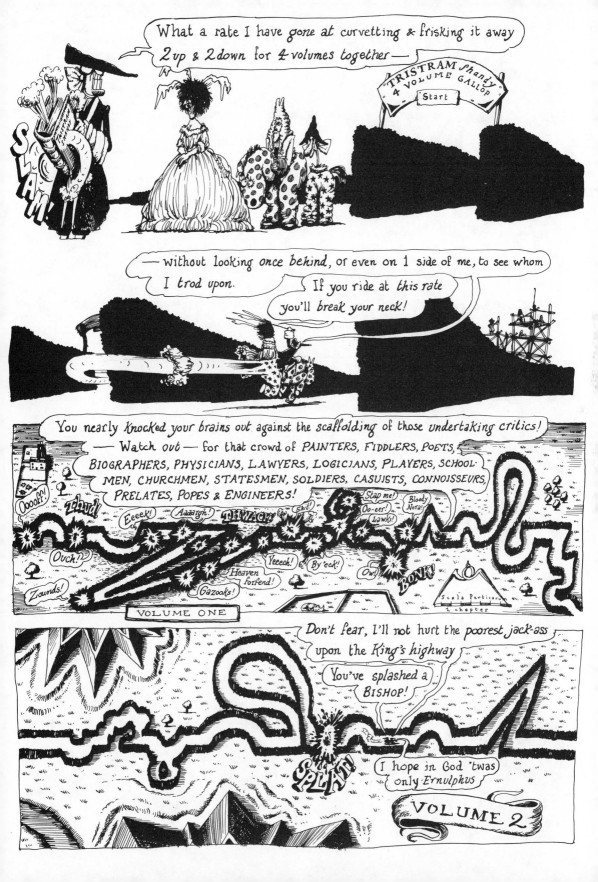

THE NEXT CHAPTER

—but of all evils, holding suspense to be the most tormenting, we shall at least know the worst of this matter.

I hate these great dinners—

We want, Mr. Shandy, to find whether the name can be CHANGED or not — & as the beards of so many commissaries, officials, advocates, proctors, registers, school-divines & others are all to meet in the middle of one table, & Didius has so pressingly invited you— who in your distress would miss such an occasion? All that is requisite is to apprize Didius, & let him manage a conversation after dinner to introduce the subject—

Then my brother Toby shall go with us.

Let my old tie-wig & my laced regimentals be hung to the fire all night, Trim.

Yet, I say, wa[s]
never once in a[ll]
cile of PHUTAT[ORIUS]
brain — but th[e]
cause of his excl[amation]
lay at least a [yard]
below —

— This I w[ill]
endeavour to e[xplain]
to you with all
imaginable
decenc[y]

There was not a soul who heard PHUTATORIUS cry that
desperate monosyllable Z — ds but assumed it was the
exordium to an *oration* against YORICK —

I have undergone such **unspeakable torments** in bringing forth this **sermon** upon this occasion —— that I declare, Didius, I would suffer **martyrdom** —— and my **horse** with me, **1000** times over, before I would sit down & make such another: I was delivered of it at the **wrong** end of me —— it came from my **head** instead of my HEART, & it is for the pain it gave me that I revenge myself on it in this manner —— To preach to shew the extent of our reading —— 'Tis not preaching the GOSPEL, but OURSELVES —— For my own part, I had rather direct **5** words POINT-BLANK to the HEART ——————

Z——z——z——

Somnolentius

Kysarcius   Triptolemus   Eugenius   Gastripheres   Phutatorius

During YORICK's harangue GASTRIPHERES brought in a basket of fine roasted CHESTNUTS, knowing that *Phutatorius* specially was particularly fond of 'em —— Now when Gastripheres placed them directly before Phutatorius, ONE CHESTNUT, of more *life & rotundity* than the rest, fell out & was sent *rolling off* the table; & as Phutatorius sat straddling under — it fell perpendicularly (and PIPING-HOT) into that *particular aperture* — for which there is no *chaste* word throughout JOHNSON's dictionary — which the laws of decorum do strictly require, like the temple of JANUS (in peace at least) to be universally SHUT UP.

The genial warmth which the chestnut *imparted* was not *undelectable* for the 1st 20 or five-&-twenty seconds —

But the *heat* gradually increasing —— the SOUL of Phutatorius, together with all his ideas, his *thoughts*, his *attention*, his *imagination*, judgment, resolution, deliberation, ratiocination, memory, FANCY, with 10 BATTALIONS of animal spirits, all TUMULTUOUSLY CROWDED DOWN to the PLACE IN DANGER leaving all his *upper regions*, as you may imagine, as empty as my purse ——

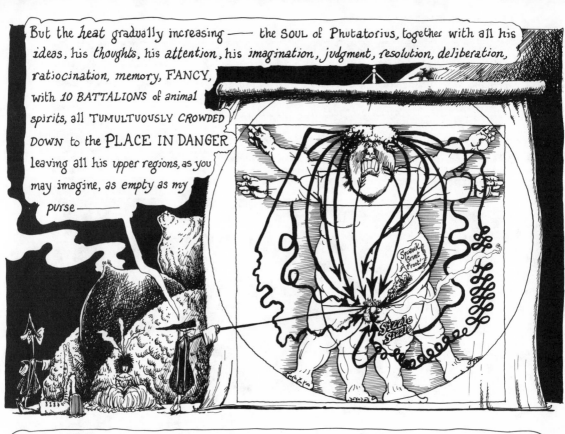

With the best intelligence which all these *messengers* could bring him back, Phutatorius was not able to dive into the secret of what was *going on* —— it might be a BITE as well as a BURN; & if so, that possibly a NEWT or an ASKER, or some such *detested* reptile, had crept up, & was *fastening his teeth* —— hence ——

ZOUNDS!!

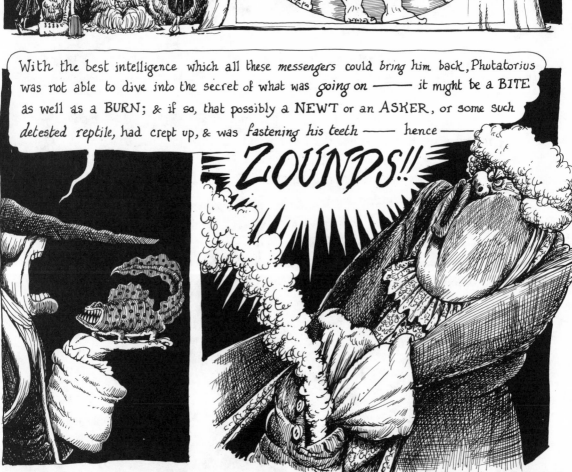

Though my father was *hugely tickled* by the *subtleties* of these learned discources — the moment he got home, the *weight* of his afflictions returned upon him when a *fresh train* of DISQUIETUDES was left him, with a legacy of *ONE THOUSAND POUNDS*, by my Aunt Dinah —

The sum was *finite* — and Nobody, but he has *felt it*, can conceive what a *plaguing thing* it is to have a man's mind *torn asunder* by 2 PROJECTS of equal strength — should my father ENCLOSE the Great OX-MOOR, or send out my BROTHER BOBBY immediately upon his *travels*?

My father had certainly *sunk under* this EVIL had he not been *rescued out of it* by a *fresh evil* — the misfortune of my BROTHER BOBBY's DEATH —

THE LAST CHAPTER of VOLUME IV

From this moment I am to be considered as *heir-apparent* to the SHANDY FAMILY — and it is from this point properly, that the Story of my LIFE & my OPINIONS sets out ———

THE
LIFE
AND
OPINIONS
OF
TRISTRAM SHANDY,
GENTLEMAN.
VOL. V.

THE

LIFE

—And such a building do I foresee it will *turn out*, as never was planned, & as never was executed since ADAM —— There will be within it *vast cazerns* filled up with *nothing*, your honours , save WHISKERS, BUTTON-HOLES, CHAMBER-POTS, SASH WINDOWS & BREECHES (with a *locked chamber* for my dear Jenny) —— and there your worships shall learn how the SHANDY *household* met the news of my brother Bobby's death & why my father wrote his great TRISTRA-PÆDIA for my education —— the story of the KING OF BOHEMIA'S CASTLES —— the ABBESS of ANDOUILLETS & her novice MARGARITA —— the Tragical Tale of the DEATH of LE FEVER (decorated at the *greatest* expense with a bespoke HIGHLY SENTIMENTAL *MISERICORD* by the RECORDING ANGEL) and —— the *choicest morsel* of my whole story!—— that part of my work taken up with the *amours* of my UNCLE TOBY in the AFFAIR of *THE WIDOW WADMAN* ——————

—————— But for *all* these you must *wait*, may it please your reverences, for the *next volume* & those *following it* when (unless this *vile cough* KILLS ME in the *mean time*) I'll lay open *all* my stories to the WHOLE WORLD.

TRISTRAM SHANDY,

GENTLEMAN.

VOL. V.

—— xero ...jocosius, hoc mihi juris Cum ...
— Si ...ur le... m decet theologum, a...t ...ordasius quam de... ...anum —— non Ego, sed ...emocritus dixit.

SO WHO ARE YOU?

OH, I'M PHILIP! I'M WRITING THE SHANDY BIOGRAPHY!

GET A MOVE ON, PETE! THIS IS WHERE IT GETS INTERESTING!

HOR.

...E...MUS.

LONDON.

Pr... by K. ALEXANDER in th...
MDCCLXVII

BLOODY HELL! WE'VE BEEN DIGITALIZED!!!

IT'S GOING TO BE AWFULLY LONG! ROY JENKINS IS WRITING THE FOREWORD

By the powers invested in me by the terms of the provisions contained within the protocols of the Oslo International Convention on HUMOUR & ITS VICTIMS, it is my duty to inform you that the Cartoon Enterprise currently being undertaken by you and/or your agents contains GROSS VIOLATIONS of existing statutary & voluntary guidelines on offensive or derogatory depictions or portrayals undertaken for the purposes of HUMOUR in the following areas:—

a) THE DEPICTION of Captain TOBY SHANDY, a *disabled war veteran* suffering from POST-TRAUMATIC STRESS DISORDER, in a *humorous, whimsical* & therefore DEGRADING FASHION;

b) The concomitant offence & distress caused to the DISABLED, especially the *urologically challenged* or *genitally different*, by the ABOVE;

c) The depiction of Mr. WALTER SHANDY, a retired *old folkperson*, as FAT, in a manner calculated to be deeply offensive to the *alternatively thin*;

d) The *highly* abusive portrayal of DR. SLOP, a ROMAN CATHOLIC, in a manner guaranteed to be deeply, deeply HURTFUL to ALL MEMBERS of ALL FAITHS, and to send *tiny children* home from school *in tears*;

e) As (d), in the abusive & *degrading* portrayal of the Holy Office of the Inquisition, & by inference all committed & orthodox members of ALL faiths, and *none*;

f) As (d), in the derogatory portrayal of the gynaecological profession in particular, and the medical & *all* other professions *in general*;

g) The wholly, *completely* & UTTERLY *UNFORGIVABLE* depiction as supposedly *humorous* of the LITANY of ABUSE, NEGLECT & MALTREATMENT suffered by an *innocent babe* through OBSTETRIC, SPIRITUAL & PARENTAL oversight, misdiagnoses or maltreatment, when *everyone knows* such things are not even *remotely funny*;

h) Further to (g) above, the subsequent *mutilation* of the child seen as a fit subject for *humour*, when it obviously isn't (see also (b) above);

i) The inadequate or minor rôle given to environmental concerns throughout the work;

j) The *childish* implication that GENDER CONGRESS is in some way or other funny, and the concomitant offence this causes all children by association, which is a *terrible thing* in itself;

k) The *frivolous* manner in which the *deathing & birthing* processes are portrayed *throughout*, when these are both very, really & truly beautiful *life odyssey* embarkation points in a very real spiritual sense;

l) The inclusion of a *lavatory* in the work, in clear contravention of all existing guidelines on the use of scatalogical material calculated to be *highly* offensive to victims of *colonic misadventure*, anal retentives and everyone else, and opening by association PLUMBERS to ridicule, calumny, opprobrium and the very real danger of *vigilante-style* VIOLENT ATTACK;

m) The vile, sick & disgustingly ABUSIVE portrayal of a WHALE, a *harassed mammal of the deep* and ambassador for ALL LIFE on PLANET EARTH.

In the light of all this, I have NO OPTION but to IMPOUND the said work to be hereafter, as accomodated for in the guidelines, BURNT IN AN ENVIRONMENTALLY FRIENDLY WAY by a specially selected group of *young people* chosen by means of a competition to compose the best haiku with the title "We are the Spirit of the Forest", organised in association with THE BODY SHOP.

Moreover, as my firm also represents your publishers, I must draw your attention to your failure to deliver this work by the date specified in the Contract (that is, some 17 years ago), which failure has resulted in my clients invoking PENALTY CLAUSE XXXVII (5)(iv) of the contract, sub-heading "Selling the Family of the Author(s) into Slavery: Options thereon".

The corporal had already — what with *cutting off the ends of my uncle Toby's spouts* —— hacking & chiselling up the sides of his *leaden gutters* —— melting down his *pewter shaving-basin* —— he had that *very* campaign brought no less than *8 new* BATTERING CANNONS, besides *3 demi-culverins*, into the field; my uncle Toby's demand for *2 more pieces* had set the corporal to work again —

Shcricenk

—— & no *better* resource offering, he had taken the 2 *leaden weights* from the *nursery window*; & as the SASH PULLIES, when the *lead* was *gone*, were of no kind of use, he had taken *them* away also, to make a *couple of wheels* for 1 of their carriages —

AHEM —

Now, there is *nothing* in this world I *abominate* WORSE, than to be *interrupted* in a STORY —

Swish

Lord! I cannot look at it —
What would the world **say** if I looked at it?
I should **drop down,** if I looked at it —
I **wish** I could look at it —
There can be no **sin** in looking at it.
— I **will** look at it.

— Some 30 toises from the returning angle before the Gate of St. Nicholas —

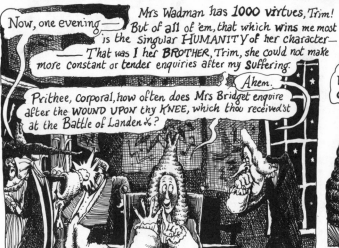

Now, one evening —

Mrs Wadman has **1000** virtues, Trim! But of all of 'em, that which **wins** me most is the singular HUMANITY of her character — That was I her **BROTHER,** Trim, she could not make more constant or tender enquiries after my suffering.

Ahem.

Prithee, corporal, how often does Mrs Bridget enquire after the WOUND UPON thy KNEE, which thou received'st at the Battle of Landen ✕ ?

She **never,** an please your honour, enquires after **it at all.**

That, corporal, shows the difference in the **character** of the mistress & maid. Had I suffered the same mischance, Mrs. Wadman would have enquired into every circumstance relating to it **100 times.**

God bless your honour! had your honour's Knee been shot into **10,000** splinters, Mrs Wadman would have troubled her head **as little** about it as **Bridget,** because the KNEE is such a **distance** from the main body — whereas the GROIN, your honour Knows, is upon the very CURTIN of the PLACE.

Let us go to my brother Shandy's.

My father, whose way was to force every event in nature into an *hypothesis*, by which means never man crucified TRUTH at the rate he did — had but just heard of the *difficulties* of my uncle Toby's AMOURS, & what were the secret articles which had delayed the WIDOW WADMAN's *surrender* —

That provision should be made for *continuing* the race of so *exalted* & *god-like* a Being as MAN — I am far from denying — but I still maintain it to be a PITY, that it should be done by means of a *passion* which bends down the faculties, couples & equals WISE MEN & FOOLS, & makes us come out of our caverns & hiding places more like SATYRS & 4-FOOTED BEASTS than MEN ——————

Whilst a man is free —

I know that in itself, & simply taken — like hunger, or thirst, or sleep — 'tis an affair neither *good* or *bad*, or *shameful* or otherwise — Why then, when we go about to make & plant a man, do we put out the candle, & for what reason is it, that all the parts thereof are so held to be conveyed to a cleanly mind by no language, translation or periphrasis whatever?

The act of KILLING a man, you see, is *glorious* —————— & the weapons by which we do it are *honourable* — we strut with them by our sides — we gild them — we carve them — we in-lay them — we enrich them — Nay, if it be but a SCOUNDREL CANNON, we cast an ORNAMENT upon the BREECH OF IT!

An' please your worship!

FINIS